A CERTAIN
MARVELLOUS THING

in memory
R.A.W.

JOHN POWELL WARD

A CERTAIN MARVELLOUS THING

Seren Books

SEREN BOOKS
is the book imprint of
Poetry Wales Press Ltd.
Andmar House, Tondu Road
Bridgend, Mid Glamorgan
Wales CF31 4LJ

© John Powell Ward 1993

British Library Cataloguing in Publication Data:

Ward, John Powell
A Certain Marvellous Thing
I. Title
821.914

ISBN:1-85411-086-1

All rights reserved. No part of this publication may be reproduced, stored in a retrieval system, or transmitted at any time or by any means, electronic, mechanical, photocopying, recording or otherwise, without the prior permission of the copyright holders.

*The publisher acknowledges the financial support of
the Welsh Arts Council*

Typeset in 10.5 palatino by the National Library of Wales, Aberystwyth

Cover Art: Ad Parnassum (Oil and casein on canvass 39x49) by Paul Klee
Courtesy of the Kunstmuseum, Bern

Contents

7	The Irish Sea From St Davids
9	Lucy
10	The Word-Processor
11	Spelling
12	From A Phrase By Janet Montefiore
13	Alphabet Soup At Midnight
15	Corner Of The Universe
17	In Mem
18	Elegy For A Species
20	Elegiac
21	England
22	Lights In The Fog
23	The River Giver
24	Photo
25	The Moment
26	Nature
27	The Subject
28	Elegy For The Accidental Dead
32	The Travellers
33	Night Swim
34	In The Box
36	Today (Sunday)
37	Beautiful and Sublime
38	The Way It Looks Right Now
40	The Estuary
42	Motif
43	Lingua Duplex

50	Incidental Tourist At St Mary's Credenhill
51	Henry Vaughan Observes From Wherever
52	Along The Beach
53	Up There On His Horse
54	Social Workers
55	A Swarm Of Bees
56	The A40 Wolvercote Roundabout At Oxford
58	Ichthus
59	Kinship, New Brunswick
60	Afterword
65	Acknowledgements
66	Author's Notes

The Irish Sea From St Davids

How often you stare at its face
Half-asleep knowing it makes you so.
Hypnotized by the quietist to and fro.
Helped by it drawing off restlessness.

Waves as primaeval endless re-writing.
Words slipped in, crossed out, crests toppling over
Without punctuation, a passage of water
Weighing its content; waves quoting, citing.

Some the tentative movements of the blind.
Some sewing, weaving and unravelling.
Some come in, tired from a day's travelling.
Some wave to you, are just the mind.

Some hit rock then are vertical spray.
Some are young dolphins dozing.
Some are envelopes opening, some closing.
Some launder, dry and put themselves away.

Tired now and shivering I watch it all.
There's radioactive junk out there.
To think when we were young it was pure.
Tides don't change much. They rise and fall,

Destined in their sea-sway to continue working.
Dumping is the sea's capacity itself.
Divers scratching around the continental shelf
Doing their pollution research, are just checking.

Beautiful how sea spreads out its hands and repents.
Botulism, chemicals and raw sewage. Then
By degrees next year another thing. Yet again,
Bent on exposing our newest innocence,

As we love to from time to time,
Almost we must go on challenging this place,
A spinning ball, just to survive us.
And so it will. Our children's home.

Children play on the cliff near the edge.
Could I save one, that fell by going too far?
Clamber the outcrop and haul it back from there?
Careful how you withdraw from the ledge

Of these fantasies and return to staring.
On the left, rocks sloshed by the sea's swell.
On the right, path to the saint's well.
Out front our new-seen sea weeping, uncaring.

Lucy

The word is light.
Then switched on, "light".

Sunlight is LIGHT.
Stained glass gives LxIeGwHaT.

Hidden light is (light).
Humour is ? light?

Jewels sparkle l*i*g*h*t.
Joy flashes: light!

Bowls of fruit are light.
Boy twins are light.

Light on your dear face,
Like that, is sheer grace.

The Word-Processor

My love is letters.
May they endear for ever.

It's the electron edict.
It is vernacular too.

Our way forward is talk
Or loud enunciation.

To think so is living
Two ways, science and art.

At least go to the
Ant and be amazed.

Be at one with the
Bee and the queen winging it.

Men strive for the generous law.
Me, I print sounds.

We axe the heart's
Web in all our persuasions.

Spelling

Is he still it now? Is Jesus
It now, or has it changed now? Is

Jesus still it now, King of
Jews like and the world now? Is he

King now still like they said, like we
Kids were told, is he king still of

Love now, like when in the bombs and
Later the rationing, is he son of

Man as they said or at least
Many said, or some said? Oh. He's

Not now. That's all over and done
Now, that's it then. Oh, right,

Oh, so it's over now. Oh well, it's
Over and gone now. Too bad then. Oh.

From A Phrase By Janet Montefiore

Hold this poem up to the light.
How beautifully the words shine

Like a stained glass window should.
Letters shimmer with angels' haloes.

Oh, I don't say the poem is so great.
Of course that depends on the meaning

Which we know is fully wrapped up
With the fixed words. Yet letters could

Be redeemed, make even a rose
Blush in the afternoon's bent sunlight.

Indeed he is sure (extravagently
It seems) all anguish will end

Magnetized up into language's swirl.
Method and philosophy too could be saved

Garnered in that way. We laugh, eat,
Grow, dream, desire, expire, just the same.

Alphabet Soup At Midnight

Ease at evening.
  Even the dog's bark downstairs
    Eloquent in the silence.

Finding start or no start so
  Far back that a guess
    Flounders right off;

Granting nothing, feeling there
  Grew from the tiniest dot
    Galaxies in moments,

High and half universes,
  Hanging like chandeliers in no
    Heaven — we get this:

If back to our origin
  Is a day, to earth's
    Itself is ten years:

Just so earth's diameter:
  Judging the length of our
    Journey to ensue

(Keeping quiet the first
  Kitchen, first kin, first
    Kill), you work out

London to Land's End done
  Less than thirty times
    Leaves us still tiny in

Measure by twenty-three
  Million of million
    Miles to our next-door star;

Nailparing beside France.
  No way to picture how
    Naked is our peach in such space.

One lucid girl's skeleton
 Out of dust was found.
  Or at least some bones.

Primates emerged.
 Perceptible thinking and tools.
  Perhaps caring, some art.

Questioning next,
 Quaint bird-gods, an oak,
  Quite sizeable tribes;

Religion crept in like
 Ripples on a lake,
  Round valleys and on

Sea-shores. Then, most
 Significant of all,
  Single tall men:

Tellers: Moses, Buddha,
 Tonguers: Plato, Mohammed, Christ,
  Taking on God himself,

Usurping that fearful one
 Until we absorbed
  Unity and so science,

Voided without such
 Verities in this aeon's
  Vast millennia ahead.

We doze at this late hour,
 Wondering after all
  Whether ours be the one world.

Corner Of The Universe

One theory is: we
  Are in a universe's corner,
  An alcove in a room,
  An inlet in a lake:

Stars in billions but
  Our suns are small last sparks
  On the rim, round a bend,
  Out of sight of the centre.

So light, at the edge, is rare.
  Wedged as we are, in darkness.
  When you move nearer — going
  Where the sparks seem to come from —

It flickers a little, or
  So one might imagine.
  Suns increase in number,
  Size and density. Then shadow itself

Whitens. At the very core (as
  Distant as grains of sand if
  Deserts were stretched, each grain
  Drawn out a trillion miles)

The gross everlasting conception
  Is illumination only;
  Isolate, hovers, holds good.
  Ice is white heat there.

John of Patmos saw it.
  White lamb, white raiment.
  (What else could he say?)
  Winter's colour, yet trope

Of imagination itself: not
  Consumed in fire, for it is fire.
  Colliding suns occur
  Close to the invisible.

Dante at the end saw it.
  Last steps in his climb.
  "Light so brilliant that both
  Lids of my eyes closed at it."

A core but an edge. No sense to
  Getting out further. Pluto's ice
  Green, green, like a swimmer
  Gone down into emerald water.

In Mem

(8 May 1990)

We cruised at 39,000 feet; over
Water it first seemed, but turned out
Westward Ho (well-named) with its long sea
Wall showing up like a black scar —
When the man beside me turned the page.

"Oh..." I said, rather too suddenly. Three
Obituaries was quite usual, but *John
Ormond* I had not seen, not known, for
Over a year, or so the fleeting time felt.
Out in the wool-clouds that sun gentled.

I looked across the cumulus, wondering
If we hope truly when thinking humans
Integrate, at death, with all that, or what
Iridium this cryst of stars will bring else.
It was daylight out there; as noon, as heaven.

Elegy For A Species

Sentinel's a thrush with cherry stains.
Sunbirds ink the rainbow to their backs.
Robinchat's a fluffy egg-yolk job.
Red-nosed hornbill; one-armed secateur.
Pattymillers are the kangaroo.
Perennially the life adorns the name.

Everywhere the war is being fought.
Elephants we knew of, then we knew
A polar bear, kept in a zoo, went mad.
After that the gophers have to die.
Spiders in millions blaze and burn alive.
Smoking though is only forced on rats.

Dear, dear warm things, companions, lovers, friends
Destructive creatures, dumb as we ourselves,
Treading those needles on the jungle floor,
Tumbling near, trapezing out of sight.
Lauding their planet, fondling its dear head,
Light forest-fur, and blue pacific eyes.

I've never seen those things. I saw a bat.
I took the fishing net a poaching boy
Left by the stream and trapped it, wriggling, scared.
Lions stay majestic. We live on a farm.
Summer the flying ants, and winter, voles.
Sometimes the foxes run and run and run.

One way would be to build an ark again.
Only this time to head for outer space.
Two elephants (a tusk each), two gulls oiled,
Two harpooned whales, two beetles underfoot,
A pair of battery hens, two baited bulls,
And what was left of humans, or just one.

Then one weekend, when vermin jam the city,
Tiny red pismires weaving necklaces
Round tops of empty bottles, eagles will land
Raiding the ghostly markets, lovely slugs
Crawl on computer screens, and one buck deer
Cross in Trafalgar Square — aloof and sad.

Elegiac

Seals die sad-eyed, whales writhe, fish found dead.
Species mysteriously disappear. Butterflies
Slip away, elephants and rhinos murdered.
Survivors are vermin and beautiful insects.

The atmosphere punctured like stretched rubber.
The forests wither, the lakes burst into flame.
The fuel that pampers us rainbows the air.
The dune beaches are boxed with hotels.

Yobs mob with their broken bottles, admired.
Yacht havens lilt rather softly on oil.
Yellow white black seethe loudly, too openly.
Years at a time drift, faster and faster.

Lying on the moon are a few footprints
Likely to stay exactly so for ever.
Love is a medium, a territory, an air.
Life shifts sideways, by inches in the mind.

Enormous changes are upon us, friend.
Education, the marvellous chance, was rejected.
Euthanasia an urgent and dangerous option.
Electricity, nature's last breath and pulse.

England

Everything is sucked to the middle.
Each screw is tightened, there is no give.
Elastically are stretched like a drum on
England its roads, for pairs to drive across.

If the noise goes on the people will madden.
If it stops they are bewildered, never find
Intent or objectives. There aren't sweet
Items of garden any more, the air unpronged.

Why are our skins flayed to bursting?
Will the millennium crack all open
With the force of a hatching egg?
We are scared. Why doesn't the news stop?

Never in history was there easement.
Nothing seems calm this week. Yet if every
New generation turned looking for ice
North, there'd be merely travel, merely snow.

Lights In The Fog

Visibility yards.
Villagers long indoors.

Off the Atlantic it settles
On the gorse-and-bracken hill.

Round hinges of gates and tufts
Rolls its war-zone barbed wire.

Lights in the paring fog
Loom down, each woolled

By a halo suspended
Between gravity and mystery

While wisps filter up from
Wet concrete as if a deep

Underworld were now smoking.
Unseen good demons met below.

Heaving like a ferry, our one
Hotel's decks carry bulbs

Strung out for Xmas joys.
"Saxon Inn" on its bows.

The River Giver

Simon the fisherman's oyster story,
Salmon the net in this western estuary,

Oiled tugs' hawsers to carry tarry
Coiled rope on the foredeck. Waves weave

Bashing green wharf-piles, the sin sign
"Bathing Forbidden" warns of depth death,

Salt oozing up and where mad mud
Silts bights more than perch perish.

Froth pouring loose a marine Marne
Forthwith is poisoned, soap soaks

Shellfish, whelks and hooked hake
Selfish sea-gods lured with cold cod

Around the fleet left and boat moat
Aground by the quayside Ireland intended,

Sealink cruising that channel charnel.
Seals' faces seal the literal littoral.

Pleating these craft of jetsam and flotsam
Pleads for a strength from the river giver.

Photo

Niagara Falls frozen in winter.
Nobody saw the moment happen.

Camera shot of a headlong rush
Collapsing eighty degrees below

Is what it seemed like. But true
Ice froze the power to a snail.

Stalactities of crept water
So the millionth drop was merely left

Further to run, upstream the river
Freezing already. We wondered

Where it ended, as with all ends.
We never knew where, or why, or when.

Look at those people out on the ice.
Lovely. Some climbing the north face.

The Moment

We have laid tarmac across countries,
We have flown faster than we know;
We have made journeys end where they began;
We have conquered the earth's curvature;
Why doesn't the brain shrink along with it;

It has shrunk as we speed round it,
It fills with our numbers like ants
In spring on some honey-coated lime;
In our minds are the furthest cities out
In the sunlight as though we own them.

Nothing is distant any more.
Nothing stops us tripping over each other's
Naked unfed bodies; nothing at all but
Nutrition of which there is not enough;
Nobody knows why we are here;

Only the emptiness is vacant.
"Out there" as we absurdly call it,
Ovals and oblongs and oblivions;
Of creation itself we are ignorant;
Our origin nearer than our endings.

Light, light and switches and light is left
Lessening before darkness each decade.
Lovely, lonesome light, speckled and fey;
Like buttercups wired to the webs of housing.
Linked to motorways the journey hurries.

Nature

Black people increase in number and
Beauty; yellow people always increased
Before white people; white people are
Bothered now and a little tired.
But let us love one another. For

There are too many of us by far
To make the planet ungentle again.
The method is impossible. We can't.
To flay the moment of penetration and
Travail — oh, oh no. Yet these women

Have had enough. They have borne us.
Have nursed us, housed us, held us,
Hugged us. Surely it is time for dreaming.
Home is the windows we stare from.
Huts were fine for the tall and scaled.

Animals, you are no part of the design.
Ants are, fish for a while longer
And birds so long as there is distance.
All the creation looks at the dry river,
Awaiting the outcome of the unintended.

The Subject

Everything has become a picture.
Events perform themselves, can't
Ever just shoot now from a tuber.
Each day's work an appointments diary.
Evolution has made us etceteras.

You might think we are watched.
Years back sky was a face, staring down
Yet now watching itself, the verb visible;
Youth a mere concept, a surface, a cloud;
Yams and yewtrees doctrine not growth.

Green forests exist to be lived in.
Goodness a fulfilled expectation;
Genuine regard no function of sun
Going about its business; rather, we
Grow aware of awareness, of image,

Of what was an infinite territory
Once, a small globe now; its nurture seen
On clear nights from — no, no other
Orbiting planet but from the very act
Of observing itself; of sight; of light.

Elegy For The Accidental Dead

These lines are for you, my dying darling.
Tactlessly to cry, what have we done?
Desperate to aid you saying "all is well"
Despite what for us you bravely bear.

If poetry means anything at all, language lingering
In the memory as chance of healing help,
It must be attempted. Truth standing trial,
Ingenious as it may seem, as weighed words.

Otherwise what mockery is this awful alphabet,
Obscuring all claim to express exactly
By a mere twenty-six signs the sighs
Bereaved ones emanate now, lovers and survivors.

***

Bow doors fatally open, a wave's whole whale
Borne in and slumped about the car cargo's
Hold from wall to wall. Continental containers
Hurled then rolled dizzily, drew drunken

Egregious water which greasily fouled filled and
Edged up to deck restaurants. Cafe coffee
Jogged and lurched, knives and tables tumbled,
Jagged broken glass. Then electric light left.

Black sucked them down screaming. Creamy
Bleary water swilled, backpacks and anoraks,
Shoes float in the full hull, their own ocean,
Shaved corpses capsized, food flooded.

Maybe the wreck of this daytrip's detritus
Makes careful and true a right sum somewhere.

***

Worse when one significant cigarette
Was dropped into that tube's flicked fluff
Years had gathered. No escalator escape,
Yards away was air but plywood and plaster

Incinerated and went white-hot
Incendiary-like. Took in the ticket-
Hall making steps rubber and melting metal's
Hell-hole. No place to hide, hideous

Panic rushed back down past glamorous absurd ads,
Pain as though instant. Lawyers, lorrydrivers,
Accountants, nurses, kids and temp typists
Accepting here so direfully to die.

God perhaps granted swift suffocation.
God's prudent way: the merciful miracle.

***

Horror gentler when just the wind wanders.
Hurricanes are of nature, purer power.
Nonetheless by such flung foliage
Nineteen died that dreadful night. Flashes flew as

Cables, tree-crashed, draped like knotted knitting.
Cabman died at the wheel when a crane crumbled.
Doughty elm, ash, fir, birch, beech came
Down and bedrooms saw sky. Oak broke

Horses' necks and crushed ewes. Roofs, rafters and
Houses caved in, a pier's sunk section
Drowning a girl. A toppled church spire spirited
Dawn dew in the next morning's mourning.

Gracefully a beech, falling hugely, hugged and
Gathered in dying arms its own owner there.

***

Where could iron ever hang in air?
White mist curled silkily over its wavering wing
Flowing into sunset as the nose rose.
Flames then in one engine, port petered out.

Wounded like a gull, the injured engine
Wandered gliding weirdly now, cockpit's co-pilot
Selected computer readings, the people appalled
Silently begging for decent descent.

Disappearing from radar in its swinging sweep,
Disastrously fell short at terminal tarmac
Avalanching to splinters on a main motorway.
Ambulances abundant for the dead, last lights.

Iteration tells nothing. We fall each earthward
In day and year, from sky the furthest fall.

***

Earthquake and flood, tornado, inferno,
Elements; earth, air, water and fire.
Very gently I must close this weary writing,
Violent at my impertinence, and taxing task.

Train crashes recently here three times.
Titanic shadow, thermonuclear Chernobyl.
A coach plunges in Spain, killing many.
Aberfan with its child wreaths withered.

Who did it, do we ask? Who remotely responsible?
Wondering gets nowhere, nor unreal railing.
Youth copes with loss, remorse remains.
Years gone we are still bearing the difference.

How tactless to try a pompous poem,
Hope to allay conscience by a considered
Icon you stick on a one-off urn.
I can give only a layout of letters.

Ferry them good Jesus, across the salt Styx.
Fly them to safety in your gone heaven.
Bury them under trees in the green ground.
Bring them from the fire, that their calm come.

Metaphor: *May light perpetual shine upon them.*
Mediaeval mind thus made praise prayer.
New times like ours are new in nervousness.
Now to attempt quiet grief; to say farewell.

    5.3.87   16.10.87   18.11.87   8.1.89
Zeebrugge King's Cross hurricane Kegworth
               and the others

The Travellers

Bravely we go; the safari parks, Palestine,
Bermuda, New Delhi, the great wall,
Bouncing along the runway and the jumbo
Ballooning up to sky with its spent crowd
Bemused on seats, fading teenier and teenier.

Foreign streets like homes are all mirrors.
Forty shops stare mute across at forty.
Fresh vegetables lie in the baskets,
Fellow-refugees drag their carts out,
Fatigued by the sluicing swish of our kind.

Pine trees sway in the new tempest.
Philosophy has somehow become perforated.
People watch their inner coloured film-shows
Petrified yet almost as much becalmed;
Persuaded not to leave; higher than peaks.

We might as well inspect before it's gone.
What's happening is, the whole lost
World is having a last frantic look round
While there's time, the equator's belt and
Ways of life melt before our very eyes

Like the Arctic snow. The level will rise;
Land-masses reshapen; faces and expressions turn
Lookalike as clothes and farms change places.
Landing we stroll tired to the arrival
Lounge and are searched. And they find everything.

Night Swim

When
    would summer be half as good?
The
    taste of a swim at midnight:
Immaculate,
    immersed, in the dunes and salty
Moonbeam,
    making all somehow darker
Below,
    beaching yourself like a whale,
An
    amazing moon whale. He was
Naked:
    Neptune a while, cold, distilling.

In The Box

Father, I have sinned and I confess.
For I am white, male and middle-class and

Was brought up in the south-east of England.
Wretched I turn desperately to you asking what

To do with these appalling errors. I have
Tried living in Canada five years and (oh shame,

Shame) in Wales twenty-five, running a cockney
Stepney youth club, stopping my offspring

(Both male too god forgive me) from yuppie-talk and
Bringing home their ghastly Oxbridge friends, I

Even give a percentage to selected charities.
Every day I deprave myself just the same,

And now know not where to turn. The worst
Aspect is this nauseating guilt-complex which

Makes me ape people's accents, pretend to like
Music-murder on the streets and all the time

Really just avoiding women, patronizing blacks and
Releasing aggro on youth and equals. God, it festers,

Old plants lose their blossoms (OK like men
Other parts, which in my case don't reach I

Guess), they turn brown and a nasty smell and die.
God. God. Did I really think all those Tory things

In those earlier years, and am stuck with them as
If no good feeling, no love, ever moved me? I come to

You for forgiveness, yes, but for guidance too in my
Years left, such as may be granted. The millennium

Comes nearer, the planet's population groups realign
Casually, cautiously and creatively, and old material

Declines as it should and must. Forgive my reactionary
Demeanour; it is a mere stuck groove and a worn

Lazy failure to rotate on the poor axis of flesh.
Life, as always, goes. I've had mine. Forgive, father.

Today (Sunday)

She flew away like a swan, and I,
Seeing how beautiful she was,
Sad I could never follow, stared for an

Hour. The spreadeagled hills already knew
Her, the clouds too, the lucid olive
Horizons her intelligent rains — like now

In this downpour drops pound the tarmac and
I swinging left into the lane see twenty
Iridescent toads crawl out for moisture

From the icier weather. Several were
Flattened by cars' tyres, some their legs'
Flesh severed. Why? What had they done?

Beautiful And Sublime

This is what I wanted to
Tell them and myself:
That light shines on letters.
Thus they can have shadows.

Our world is bathed in light,
Outer space is dark and all
Obscure. But ignorance being
Obscurity too, knowledge is

Light. Knowledge is exact, its
Least details are clear. When
Let there be light was said
Learning was forbidden, that tree's

Fruit to stay unpicked. When humans
Fell (as it was put) they opened
Futures for themselves in which
Furtherance of knowledge could

Become the norm; the secular was
Born. But for that reason, and
Because our world is light and
Beyond darkness, is not ignorance

Always the outer rim? Can we know
All ever? I go back to my own
Ambition here; to write and
Articulate it in words' substance.

The Way It Looks Right Now

Light shines on everything.
Lazy, lonely light, on bedsteads,
Lines of trees, and verandahs. It
Lends authority to bollards.

Oh but that barely starts it!
Opulence and shit; radios;
Open and shut doors; pyramids,
Otters and rats — the light joins all.

Sunlight that is, not mere grey
Sultry afternoon atmospherics.
Shining entails a beam. Whether on
Sugar-lumps or mountain-ranges.

Hence this light we crave can never
Hide a thing. In endless light
Heat, not truth, is what's redundant.
However, as Bacon said, a lie

Is somehow attractive, and we can't
Imagine all bare to the lamps
Incessantly. Many indeed want dark.
It just means that both cherish.

But where do all the people
Belong in this? In sunlight too?
Blacks, child-victims, women,
Buddhists, Iranians, Tibetans and Brits

Traverse the road in jeans and
T-shirt monogram; swear, eat and
Troublemake. We shiver and are
Tormented but light comes again.

And if we love it ourselves, we
Are arraigned and borne out to
An integration: we end there
Answerable, cheerful, small.

Everything joins cheerfully in light.
Each person, object and insect
Enters its trust and no grief lasting.
Even dark laughs aloud at such ending.

The Estuary

It sank into memory, this mud, as
If snow or glass lay on it, or white light

With a weird electron charge
Working, mere search getting you nowhere

On film, or in a book
Or down there in your earlier mind.

Last week, one stormy day
Late afternoon, late autumn in the sun

We saw the river's bend
White-hot, pure white below the black

Rain-clouds, making a white
Rare glow, almost as though too hot

To touch. It fused itself
Through every sentence that you spoke,

And bent round like a moon,
A grey horseshoe, a great loud meander

In the daytime. Some new
Injection of cheap housing too,

Felt its way down the bank too
Fast, to a flyover and underpass

Quite close to what the people felt,
Quietly expecting life, or bearing it.

We didn't find a thing,
What to do, what space-time is or matter

(Truths water, cloud and air are meant
To yield up of their natures),

But no success either
By face-on probe or brainwork alone;

Just that incredible shine,
Jostling the bridge and wharf-piles,

Up from the river sliding by,
Unmoved by any watching; and the people walking

On the esplanade, like handwriting,
Opening their faces to each other, then

Going back to their cars,
Given a new touch from the sky's light.

So: when one tries for "thought" from
Such things, or "life", or "environment",

All just slips from the mind
And vanishes; only when more is dreaded

Does their resting there seem
Double, like a current that eddies backwards

Oddly twisting, even when
On ebb to the barrage below. Anyway,

At last we left, wondering if all that
Appears round here, even pollution, is the same,

Castle now crumbling away,
Cathedral used up, both so old yet both

Like deer silting down to the river,
Licking the water that steered there first,

Arriving never, taking mental/chemical
Advances in its stride, or rejecting them still.

Motif

All the words broke in
Agony. They were sick and sad,
An endangered species.

For they were like
Fruit soaked with insecticide.
Figs swung to grief. They

Dared board no streetcars
Downtown or to oval stadia.
Daytime had become a pit.

Perhaps we had pushed and
Pulled them till the blood ran.
Patient tongues nursed them.

Only new film struggled
On for light, celluloid keeping
Open that raw courage.

Till one year a strange planet was
Towed into orbit opposite
To ours. Its green bloomed.

Words leapt like fish;
Whales and seals in cobalt
Water trumpeted sunshine.

Hope, said the farmer,
Hangs like season's apples we
Have bent ripening into gold.

Lingua Duplex

And she is gone.
His sedge anon,
Needs in a song,
And she is gone.

Age end his son.
Side on he sang,
One has signed
And she is gone.

One snag I shed.
Oh, gains, needs,
God has seen in
And she is gone.

Seasoned nigh,
Send a one sigh,
O ensign shade,
And she is gone.

Seeding on ash
Digs he as none?
He goes in span
And she is gone.

A tortured man,
O that I am,
Bent in a name.
Nowhere was home.

A tortured man,
O that I am,
A tot, a him,
Bent in a name.

Bent in a name.
A tin man been.
How we see no harm.
Nowhere was home.

He worse he woman
Nine-beat man
Mandate or rut.
O that I am.

***

1) his stormy herd helped: that sin won all

2) deer awaken to morning; his the mute sleep:
   wealth is idle, see the deaths tremble

3) or myths rouse Lethe. darkness heals the emotions, pet rage,
   the hashish menu is off;

4) the lark died halfway to heaven; Eve hollow girl, at the
   fight oh how you fail us;

   watch my deft foot, the sound of rhythm, fair to the martyr;

5) riper than a tree fount in blossom, ephebe, free enemies met
   peace:

   who, hip autumn city? the day returns, the moon in love;

6) dodge eye, fly home, world's lonely music falls, harmony's
   last leaf;

   old field shire fell, and nowhere without lover.

                                                    (Psalm 23)

***

That you will note is an anagram.
The same letters in different positions.
Of course, the second always sounds awkward.
Lucky overcrowding is less fuss.

Still an amateur tho', no way gain.
Finesse stint, meteors, half-pint editors.
As we who understand, cool red sky was a focus
Scurrying cooks slugs, few lived

*

Good poetry today is vernacular.
bleedin shit fuckin cunt bleedin ell.
He anagrammed it nine times at Paddington.
Louder and louder.
Louder, louder and louder.

British Rail Paddington
Air bird sand point light

William Shakespeare
seek a wall, praise him

those twenty-six letters
text, show, interest, style

true mind rudiment
ABC is basic

certainly neat lyric
chiasmus has music

*

Lake District
trick details

Welsh Tourist Board
showed tribal routs

Oxford and Cambridge
add red BA from coxing

there is no woodland
one H-world instead

sectional coastline
no men invent environment

nostalgia lost again
another on earth

a theology of people and the planet
elephant, pony, pelt, hoof, toad, eagle

same thoughts turn present
greatness thrust upon them

Terry Waite
a writer yet

Mother Teresa
O rarest theme

***

Government loyalty undermined from the start
Government loyalty underlined from the start

Not particularly the dates
Note particularly the dates

The homeless want to buy a house
The homeless went to buy a house

They will punish cruelty without compassion
They will punish cruelly without compassion

Race appears to race to forbear
Race appeals to race to forbear

***

All must be seen,
  Tell, see as numb,

Psyche outward
  Cheaty words up

Telegraph loves
  All over the pages

The stitching shows
  Which ghost isn't set;

Toilets and shit
  Last on this tide

Black yellow white red
  It wrecked hello by law

Become rage not walk,
  We cram a token globe,

Nimby crank today,
  Not in my back yard.

By far we are too many
  We are too many by far

*

O friend stop moaning!
No id-foe past morning

Why, how can I sing this?
Wish, wich, say nothing

Observe, pleb peacemonger
Bare people becoming verse

Her ire urges deterrent sense
Green trees need their users

History sweeps wrath, fan told
For the windows play the stars

***

split ghost, her engulf it all, wept on reprisal,
sink prose, a rook could, rose flux Gaia,
able champ, begin Chester, sits in hunger,
education's far ray, earls, to its perch,
car fuse, bio-warn, filled hot growth,
hang steel, incandescent hill sigh zigzag north

spotlights, in the full glare, ripples on water,
pink roses, Kodacolour, four galaxies,
Palm Beach, the big screen, the rising sun,
your radiant faces, laser, the tropics,
surface, rainbow, light of the world,
the angels, an intense scorching dazzling light

                                          for then lamps create
                                          the last performance

fuel vice, join strength
  the curving jet flies on

plainly to use
  easy to pun ill

a gender enraged
  seek a man's namesakes

noon miners bleed but wilt
  buried not ten miles below

enter at last the poor, the needy
  then restore the planet one day

Incidental Tourist At St Mary's Credenhill

I leave, then see the note enjoining us
To pray for ourselves but also those who worship
And minister here. Uncertain I return,
Finding my car-key underneath the pew.
O god help all, ill, RAF, the strong.

I prayed for them. I didn't do it well.
The need to laze in the churchyard grew.
Ah! There were apples too, I was discreet.
Facing all things with a little wit
One deals with moralists, and sin.

Inject that psychiatric strength
They say you have, "green nature", into me
And I won't weep at twilight any more.
Fear's dismal melancholy, scary trees
Obscure in shadow, the unplanned hills

Interred in fields that do no wrong,
Trespass on guilts that kill my life
As sleeping-pills of night fail to restore
Faintheartedness of days. The sweet damp stone
Odouring the church smells good, yet I'd cave in

If I stayed here. Then I read these words:
"That corn was orient and immortal wheat
 And never should be reaped, nor was ever sown."
Found in a pamphlet. How their rhythm sang
Of some unanswered world, stranger than mine.

Henry Vaughan Observes From Wherever

I saw eternity the other night
In a great ring of pure and endless light,

London orbital emm twentyfive
Lilting and twining on its wounded curve

Beatifically shrunk from my dark above.
Below is where persons sleep and live,

Hairdressers, tombs, cheap sex, gardens,
Heathrow for a time in geometry's pylons,

Filtering through the deep terrain's scar.
Fields' stamps, quarries, the wet windsurfer.

Clockwise and anticlockwise spins my clock,
Counting down the century's end on tarmac.

Along The Beach

The sand spreads wide,
Trillion-particled.
Teeming and crushed in
To bits by salt water.

Some swirls to form.
Such is the ribbed shore
Sea daily fondles,
Shaping it in curves.

Other are stretched
Of grain and grain only.
Ordinals gathered
On self and more self.

Now here's something new!
No ocean's ravage or
Numb distance; plain
"Nicky and Teresa",

Distinguishably scrawled,
Damp toe-marks lying. Someone
Drew that, we say; someone
Dear to someone else.

Millions multi-coloured.
Mauve-tic'd, faceted,
Magenta, beryl, opal
Mackerel maybe, flecked-red.

Up There On His Horse

The holly with its brilliant berries of blood.
The footprint lying in the centuries' snow.

Des Dolan sits up there on his horse
Downing punch at the Boxing Day meet in the morning.

He is Master of the Hounds in his red coat.
Hegel looked up at Napoleon once

Like that, numbed at the arsenal of power
Locked on one saddle, out in the agora.

Once he nearly played rugby for Ireland.
Only the selectors determined otherwise.

Ants suffer, and mice do, and petrels, and fish.
And all God's creatures in their kind.

Social Workers

Call to order. Nice to see one or two
New faces (on such a drizzly evening
Too ha-ha.) Thanks Joan for sorting it out
With Catering. Someone called Les it seemed
Was butt of allusion, himself not there.
"Vote please to keep the same venue?" Same venue.
The usual iron pipes for the central heating
With a red wheel like a ship's tiny helm.

Coffee cups. Clubroom tubular chairs
And formica tables. District Committee
For the Blind; the treasurer's report,
Hardly inspiring, and yet one somehow guessed
At domestic heroics inside her. Bill, Shirley.
Jokes (the male is inferior). Old dear
With her careful white stick, eyeballs rolling,
Golden retriever. Reminded us why we were there.

Suddenly, a light, *a fucking great snow
White light*, pierced a huge hole in the ceiling,
A shaft of neon penetrating the steel girders,
Down past plywood and Roman-numeral clock,
On to the table, more blazing than sun itself,
An upright laser beam where dolphins danced,
A furnace white that crushed us, each and all,
Like a pillar of snow. Then it was gone.

There was total silence. They were so stunned they
Turned, momentarily, to salt. Only a titter
Gently dissolved the strange unlasting dream
Of oblong doors and circular plastic flowers,
Restoring the humdrum, the anecdotal, the everyday.
One wrinkled lady who had to be included.
The strong chairman finding herself impatient.
A bloke who slightly got on her wick.

A Swarm Of Bees

Random flying bees shot round
Their nucleus like electrons wound
In orbits on an atom's mind.

The population of a town.
A punchball hanging upside down.
A huge ripe pear, a buzzing one.

They crawled, as on each other's mat,
Or like on some tweed overcoat
Where stitching's come alive, not flat.

An expert came and tip-toed up
To shake the curved branch to the top
Neatly and make the whole swarm drop

Like a gold studded brooch in air,
Into a grocer's carton where
As with a splash to disappear

Completely, though there still were some
Delayers, bees that dribbled from
The box's side like liquid, gum.

The bees flew quietly round and round.
At midnight, TV changed the sound.
By satellite the camera panned

Up from the U.S. Superbowl,
Up, up through the night until
The stadium was a swarm of small

And helmeted men, gold at midnight,
The opponent team in blazing white
Like light, like intellectual light

That Dante saw, too bright to see.
Still from our loaded apple tree
Pure gold dripped from the honey bee.

The A40 Wolvercote Roundabout At Oxford

"O" the ubiquitous, the wheel.
A while if only for a while.
A lawn reflecting orange light.
A helipad whence to depart.

Why is he restless? Moons about,
Disturbs the static April night?
O the ubiquitous prayer-wheel,
The ring of lamp-posts tapering tall.

"Welcome to Scholars' Oxenford"
And watch the town roulette-wheel speed
Its bits of centrifugal thought
Off at all angles to the night

As cars brake to its edge, then yield
To let a prior group roar ahead
Then move themselves, or tucked behind
Swing to an exit out beyond,

An arc of concentrated thought.
He paced a little, sensed them do it,
Sat on a civic bench to watch
Them merge and hesitate, guess which

Split-second move a car would make
So miss some other overtake
Some other. None of them remained
More than an instant in his mind,

Not knowing what each driver bore
Most deeply, fears, obsessions, for
Those shed, like clothes, they dropped away
For one lone vagrant passer-by

Witnessing all their stop-start game.
He only saw them go and come
Lane-dodging, weaving, and the wheel
Their curvings made contain them all

As persons, work to suck them in
To this spun centre with its own
Illuminata, then away
To "Stratford, The North", infinity

Ichthus

Belief is commoner than before. Now

Leaves on the tree are falling in

Autumn's sunlight as on the goldilocks of

Christ. The jew was (you may have read)

King and fished in all the filthiest canals.

Kinship, New Brunswick

I went, in a great fall of
snow, to the airport, and trudged across
the tarmac, wrapping my coat tight
round me, and lightly met the silver
plane with my fingers, it being so
cold that they seized into solid
metal, and I took my seat, and we took
off and flew, we passengers with our
cold food and iced drinks, to an unthinkable
height, so that the plane was one
speck of dust blown over a cold compound,
scaling the sea to a far
coast, barren with frozen lakes,
fir trees, and deep snow, and we came
down, five hundred miles later, over the
huge river of ice-floes, to a city, and
I took another plane, flew to a town, an outpost
where the people lived, with shovels, to
dig out their sidewalks of the snowfall, and
I entered the icicled house, and stayed
with the two old people, and peered, through a
sheet-glass window, at the flat space of snow
and the white park, a Christmas scene, and
there was utter silence, and ice gripped
the earth, and breath itself was as
if metal, and those two old people,
their eyes were buttons, their mouths coke,
and they were as careworn, as brave, as the ice
in the dog's bowl, and I went outside, my boots
in the printed snow, by the pine trees,
watching a plane take off, from the
airstrip, myself staring, at that white depth
of parabolic drift, that deep crust of pines.

Afterword

"We can date the origin of the North Semitic alphabet, or of its prototype, which we can call proto-Semitic alphabet, in the second quarter of the second millennium BC. In other words, the great event occurred probably in the Hykson period, which is now commonly dated 1730-1580 BC. There is no doubt that the political situation of the Near East in that period favoured the creation of a "revolutionary" writing, a script which we can properly call "democratic" in distinction from the "theocratic" scripts of Egypt, Mesopotamia or China."

"The fact that alphabetic writing has survived with relatively little change for three and a half millennia, notwithstanding the introduction of printing and the typewriter, and the extensive use of shorthand writing, is the best evidence for its suitability to serve the needs of the whole modern world. This simplicity, adaptability and suitability has secured the triumph of the alphabet over the other systems of writing."
> David Diringer *The Alphabet: A Key to the History of Mankind* (Hutchinson 1947, pp. 37 and 214)

"Unlike other forms of writing, the alphabet seems to have been invented only once, and to have spread rapidly to other cultures."

> Richard M.Warren, 'Perceptual basis for the evolution of speech', pp. 101-110 in *The Genesis of Language*, ed. Marge E. Landsberg, Mouton, The Hague, 1988.

***

Could there have been a wholly different alphabet? Or could our own alphabet be seen as infinite, just as the rainbow, supposedly containing "seven" colours, really has thousands if the microscope goes in close enough? Does amalgamating letter-combinations make for all the sounds that the movements of our brains and emotions could ever need?

Writing's great part in the standardization of the major languages came with the invention of paper and then print. Copies could be distributed and speech became, or remained, diversified. Now, with radio, sound TV, tape-recorder and telephone, it is speech that can be distributed while writing becomes diversified by the artwork that preys upon it. Written language breaks up with the freedom of the adman: letters fly through the sky, go into a mad spin, shine through petrol or lager, are slit down the middle, make the frames of photographs, come in different colours and print-faces. Crossword puzzles, shopfronts, T-shirts, ads, headlines, logos, acronyms, puns: different typeface, mixed typeface, typeface suggesting luxury, chaos, fragmentation, power, classical decorum, the cigarette brand name crumbling on the sea bottom, the perfume seen through the glass of the bottle, the silly estate agent's name falling off the end of the shelf: Esso, Kelloggs K, QASAR, CBI, USA.

Letters are made of twigs, limbs, grit, icicles, electricity, splinters of glass, blades of grass, bones; individual daisies in a whole landscape, flowers, insects, petals. The lyric poem is soaked in letter-sounds, and swims inside their liquid chances.

***

"Graphomania, a sanguine faith in the calligraphic or, better still, typographic sign and its time-defeating fixity, was one of the acuter forms of semiotic credulity manifested in esoteric circles."
Keir Elam

"Writing, though unrelated to its inner system, is continually used to represent language. We cannot simply disregard it."
Ferdinand de Saussure

"*Colour expresses something itself;* one cannot do without this, one must use it." Vincent Van Gogh

"The poetic function (of language) projects the principle of equivalence from the axis of selection into the axis of combination".

Roman Jakobson

***

In China it is still an honour to be asked to "write the title" of a friend's book or dissertation. The honoured person then actually writes it, with black ink and a brush.

A traditional belief existed that there was a letter missing from the alphabet in the Torah, to be restored in the next Shemittah.

***

BEAUTY

A) Beauty is unique. As in sport, you couldn't have the identical game twice, not even by copying.

B) Beauty is not desirable. Desire is always for a lack, as Wordsworth and Freud saw. Beauty makes for desire for something else.

C) Beauty cannot be consumed.

Some passages:

The aesthetic has no concept.
    (Immanuel Kant *Critique Of Judgement*)

We love we know not what, and everything allures us.
    (Thomas Traherne)

Beauty is perfect, and perfection (such is human nature) holds our attention but for a little while...Beauty is a blind alley.
    (Somerset Maugham, *Cakes And Ale*, chapter XI)

    Much as he would like to
    Concentrate completely
    On the precious Object,
     Love has not the power:
    Goethe put it neatly;
    No one cares to watch the
    Loveliest sunset after
     Quarter of an hour.

  (W.H. Auden, 'Heavy Date')

The present object shall give you this sense of stillness that follows a pageant which has just gone by. But who can go where they are, or lay his hand or plant his foot thereon?...Is it that beauty can never be grasped?"   (Emerson, *On Nature*)

We are moved by that which always eludes us. We cannot mingle with the splendours we see.
    (Richard Harris, *Independent* 4 Feb 1990)

Anything in any way wise beautiful or noble owes the beauty to itself, and with itself its beauty ends; praise forms no part of it; for praise does not make its object worse or better.
    (Marcus Aurelius)

    ***

DEAR MOTHER

As you said, it would have been his birthday,
August the twenty-fourth. We sat in Hereford hearing

Britten's *Requiem* with Wilfred Owen's songs and
Both felt the gasp of vaults with that huge

Cathedral ceiling hung over us. Please don't
Cry any more, I miss him but know his presence

Daily now, his beliefs yes but his cheer most of all.
Deliverance, he said. Disease of the mind

Entrapping the nearest and dearest, to the very
End. He wrote me five letters last year.

***

Because I have a marvellous thing to say,
A certain marvellous thing.
      (W.B. Yeats)

***

Acknowledgements

Some of these poems have appeared in *Acumen, Bete Noire, New Welsh Review, Oasis, Orbis, Other Poetry, Planet, Poetry Durham, Poetry Ireland Review, Poetry London Newsletter, Poetry Review, Poetry Wales, The Rialto* and *Staple;* also *The Bright Field:* Carcanet's Anthology of Contemporary Poetry From Wales, *The Collins Anthology of Contemporary Christian Poetry* and *The Hutchinson Book of Post-War British Poets.*

Author's Notes

The poem 'Corner of the Universe' is based on an article which appeared in the *New Scientist* a few years ago.

The poem 'Incidental Tourist at St Mary's Credenhill' refers to the church in Herefordshire where Thomas Traherne was rector in the seventeenth century. There is an RAF training centre in the village of Credenhill.